THE BEGINNING OF
THE END

THE BEGINNING OF THE END

DRAGON APPROVED™ BOOK ELEVEN

RAMY VANCE

MICHAEL ANDERLE

DISRUPTIVE IMAGINATION

THE BEGINNING OF THE END TEAM

Thanks to the JIT Readers

Kathleen Fettig
Diane L. Smith
Deb Mader
Kerry Mortimer
Veronica Stephan-Miller
Kelly O'Donnell

If we've missed anyone, please let us know!

Editor
The Skyhunter Editing Team

Copyright © 2021 by Ramy Vance & Michael Anderle
Cover Art by Jake @ J Caleb Design
http://jcalebdesign.com / jcalebdesign@gmail.com
Cover copyright © LMBPN Publishing
A Michael Anderle Production

LMBPN Publishing
PMB 196, 2540 South Maryland Pkwy
Las Vegas, NV 89109

First US Edition, May 2020
Version 1.01, February 2021
eBook ISBN: 978-1-64202-928-4
Print ISBN: 978-1-64202-929-1

DEDICATION

To Martha Carr ... thank you for helping get on board this crazy train!

—Ramy

*To Family, Friends and
Those Who Love
to Read.
May We All Enjoy Grace
to Live the Life We Are
Called.*

— Michael

CHAPTER ONE

Alex stared in horror at the yawning portal resting above the Earth, from which emerged an ensemble of horrors. Vrosks with their mangy feathers, bizarre technological experiments hanging from the creature's beaks. A ship that stretched back into the portal, a horrid thing that looked to be made of flesh, covered in windows that might have been its eyes. Tendrils adorned its bow as if it were some perverse squid shot out into the dark, uncaring black of space.

The dragonriders had stopped in their tracks. They couldn't move forward, not after having seen the abominations crossing into their plane of existence. All they could do was stare in growing terror, a terror that was radiating from that ship as if it had been weaponized. "What the hell is that thing?" Brath shouted.

Alex would have answered, but she felt like her head was splitting open. A familiar voice had wormed its way into her head—the Dark One. He had spoken to her once before, aboard the meteor. Now he was speaking again. A few moments earlier, he had told her that Vardis was not to be trusted. Since then, Alex's head had been full of white noise, a meandering sort of thought. "It's the Dark One," she finally managed.

Gill, who was flying beside Alex and Chine, whirled around to meet Alex's eyes. She could see fear in them. "Wait, are you saying *the* Dark One?" he asked. "Aboard the ship?"

Alex nodded, certain for reasons she couldn't put into words that the Dark One was aboard that ship. Not one of the different incarnations like the pale white child; the real deal was on that ship, and he'd come for Alex.

"Alex, what's the plan?"

She couldn't tell who had asked. Everyone seemed far away at the moment. Her head was pounding, and she was having a hard time putting her thoughts together. If she had any thoughts. She wasn't certain what she was doing so far above the Earth.

The dragonriders sat there dumbly as the Dark One's forces continued to pour out of the portal like a foul oil spill across the ocean.

Brath's voice rang out over the comm. "We need to move now!" he shouted. "Everyone on me! Someone wrangle Alex!"

Gill and Jim spun around Alex so that they could force her backward, away from the portal opening.

Whatever was affecting Alex was affecting Chine as well. The dragon's joints were locked as if he had been scared motionless. If the two hadn't been breathing, it would have been easy to assume they were dead.

Jim, Gill, Jollies, and Vardis followed Brath as he retreated toward the far side of the moon, but he didn't stop there. He headed toward an asteroid field beyond it. He set down on one of the asteroids, and the dragonriders descended beside him.

Brath leaped off Furi and came over to Alex, who was muttering to herself, holding her head in her hands. "Hey! Alex?" he shouted.

Alex looked up, hardly able to keep her eyes on him. They kept moving back and forth as if she were looking for something. She could see Brath, but something about him being in front of her didn't make any sense.

The white noise was still drumming in the back of her head. Suddenly, it surged to a crescendo, hitting a fever pitch as a voice screamed, "Alex!"

Alex twitched violently as if she had been shocked and jerked upward. Her body relaxed as she stared into space, trying to make sense of the vague waves of information pouring through her head from the Dark One's ship.

Jollies flew to Alex and tugged on her cheek, to no avail. "Is she going to be okay?" the pixie asked the assembled crew.

Brath looked over his shoulder to see if the Dark One's forces had followed them. "I have no idea, but we can't wait for her to stop freaking out to figure out what to do. Otherwise, we're all going to end up dead."

Gill, who had knelt beside Alex, asked Brath, "What do you think we should do?"

"We can't risk a head-on fight. We're way outnumbered. If we charge them, we're just going to end up dead."

"Astute observation. We could hide."

The asteroids would make a reasonable hiding place. The field looked to be too densely populated for the Dark One's flagship to follow them in. The vrosks would have the ability to weave in and out of the asteroids, but so would the dragonriders. That would at least put them all on the same playing field.

Figuring out what to do was the most important thing. Luckily, Alex had never been much of the planner until recently. Everyone in Boundless was used to making deci-

3

sions. "If we hide here, we could be easily overrun," Jollies squeaked. "We can't just stay still."

Gill paced as he tried to think of something. "We could all take different positions," he suggested, pointing to three different spots that formed a triangle. "We could attack from above and below, cutting out some of the vrosks. We still won't have to deal with the ship. Once we get the numbers down, we can funnel them to a kill spot."

Jim had exited his mech and now was walking up the asteroid, checking for different vantage points. "That's not a bad idea. We could have the heavy hitters down here, pounding them with artillery, and two lighter Riders up at the top."

Boundless was in survival mode. There was no way they were going to be able to outrun the forces they had seen coming through the portal, and there could be more.

Jollies pointed to an asteroid off to the left, and she and Amber headed toward it. Gill did the same. Brath and Jim stayed behind with Alex, who was starting to come out of the fog of the Dark One's influence. "He's here!" Alex muttered as she tried to get to her feet. "He's actually here."

Jim helped Alex get up and held her steady as she stumbled. "Don't you hear him?" she asked, her eyes wide and frantic. "Can't you hear him?"

"I don't hear anything," Jim told her.

Suddenly, Alex fell to her knees, gripping her skull as she screamed, "He's in my head! He's in my head!"

Brath and Jim exchanged glances, neither of them knowing what to do in the situation. They could tell Alex was in pain but didn't know how to help. "Chine, is there anything you can do?" Jim asked the dragon.

Chine didn't respond. His eyes had rolled back in his head and smoke was coming from his nostrils, but he paid no attention to the human or the gnome. "Guess we gotta figure this one out on our own," Brath muttered.

Jim guided Alex over to Chine and sat her down by the dragon's feet. "She'll come out of it," the mech rider said. "Something like this happened on the meteor. She's linked to the Dark One. I don't know how, but it happened. They went into some kind of vision or alternate reality. It's hard to understand, but the two of them are linked."

"Like her and Vardis."

Jim glanced at the alien, who was standing away from everyone else as if he were waiting for something. "Yeah," Jim said slowly. "Like with Vardis."

Brath grimaced. "Your girlfriend seems like she's been getting the raw end of everything. Lucky she's so tough."

"She's not my—"

The gnome shrugged. "You stay close to her. I'll move up and take point. Furi should be able to handle whatever comes this way. Just make sure nothing happens to her."

Brath walked toward Furi and leaped onto his back, leaving Jim there with Alex, who could barely comprehend what was going on around her. If she had been aware, she wouldn't have believed the amount of respect Brath had shown toward her, but that was most likely why Brath had said it. He knew Alex wouldn't hear.

Jim got back into his mech, bringing it around to Alex and Chine and preparing for the vrosks that were going to come through the asteroids at any minute. He was trembling, staring at the stars and asteroids around him.

Alex watched all of this happening, feeling as if she were both present and someplace far away. The Dark One's voice was still ringing in her ears, although now it made less sense. She couldn't tell if he was speaking to her or if she was merely hearing whatever constituted his thoughts.

Chine stretched his wing over Alex as he curled into a ball, pulling her closer to him. Alex was glad the dragon was here with her. Even though she didn't know specifically what he was doing, she could feel him fighting something off. Maybe he was the only reason she wasn't going insane.

The rest of Boundless was secured in their positions. Now they were simply waiting. Silence and tense nerves as the vrosks and whatever else could have come from that portal were heading toward them. "Anybody know a good joke?" Jollies finally asked.

Brath was scratching the back of Furi's neck, trying to soothe the dragon, who was just as stressed as everyone else. "One that pixies would find funny?" he asked. "Is it even a joke? You all laugh at just about anything."

"Then it shouldn't be hard for you to think of one, right?"

Gill and Jim snickered over the comm, and Brath turned nearly as red as his beard. "Okay, I got one," Brath said. "A gnome and a drow walk into a bar. The bartender asks, 'What will you two be having?' The gnome says, 'Whatever you got on the menu.' The bartender turns to the drow and asks, 'What about you?' The drow leans over the bar and says, 'Your finest stones.'"

Nobody laughed. The silence grew thicker and thicker. "Uh, I think jokes are supposed to be funny," Jim teased.

Brath shouted, "Gnomes don't do humor, all right!"

Gill was snickering, barely able to manage, "It's kinda impressive. You managed to say something a pixie didn't think was funny."

Amber set off a small electrical pulse and Jollies quipped, "You're right. There was nothing funny about that."

"Gnomes don't tell jokes!" Brath shouted again. "Wait, hold up, guys. I think they're coming."

Boundless looked at the stars, which were twinkling like

lost dreams. In the distance, they could see the vrosks massing. The attack was beginning.

The dragonriders readied their weapons. This was going to be a fight worth remembering—if they survived.

CHAPTER TWO

Jollies and Gill headed toward their positions, leaving Jim and Brath on the asteroid with Alex, waiting for the Dark One's forces to make it to them. Jim hovered over Alex as she slipped in and out of consciousness. Whatever was happening was getting worse.

Brath didn't know what to do. He felt completely unprepared for the situation. Even though he had started everyone talking about a plan, he'd been surprised to hear himself speak. Giving orders wasn't his thing. It wasn't that he liked following them. Responsibility wasn't his thing either.

That didn't matter at the moment. All of the Riders were responsible for Alex. She'd placed her life on the line way too many times for them to let anything happen to her. The only reason any of them were still alive was because of her.

Alex screamed again, and Brath wished it was true that no one could hear you scream in space. She sounded like she was in pain, and it was very obvious that there was nothing any of them could do about it.

Vardis was standing far from the rest of the group. He was staring at the moon as if he could see something.

Brath had to fight the urge to walk up behind Vardis, pull him down, and beat the living snot out of him. He didn't trust the guy. The whole situation with the kin attacking them had been ridiculous. What was supposed to be a simple mission had turned into a disaster, and Vardis was possibly responsible for it.

Maybe he's working with the Dark One, Brath thought. *This could have all just been an orchestrated double-cross.*

As Brath watched Vardis, that possibility seemed less likely. If Vardis was working with the Dark One, then why was he still with Boundless? He should have bounced as soon as the Dark One's forces had shown up.

Brath didn't even want to think about the amount of firepower they were going to be up against. It was hard for him to fathom that the Dark One had come to the battle in person. Actually, it was horrifying. All of the nine realms had been fighting this guy's armor, and almost no one had ever seen or heard him. Except on the gnome world.

The memories came faster than Brath was prepared for. The smell of burning flesh, the screams that never ended, that seemed to stretch across the entire planet. Weeks without food, scouring in the forest like animals being hunted.

Gnomes had seen the Dark One. Many of them were now dead. Brath was lucky to have escaped when the gnomish world fell, but others hadn't been as lucky. Not the ones who had seen the Dark One's face.

Stories had been shared between survivors. Brath never talked about his own. No one needed to know what had made him an orphan. But he listened to everyone else's tales. He'd memorized them, carved them into his heart. He internalized the pain of every gnome he met and swore revenge.

One gnome he remembered, not much older than him, had spoken about how she had seen the Dark One's actual

9

face. She'd been part of the early resistance that had fought when the Dark One's first ships touched down on the planet. Her squad had been mostly wiped out. The rest had been captured.

She said she'd been brought into a throne room, and that was where she had seen him. His face never rested, like it was made of black water, constantly shifting and changing. Sometimes it was the face of a friend. Other times it was her own. Then it would become something much worse—a deep emptiness that sent her spiraling into madness for weeks to come.

No one ever asked the gnome how she'd escaped. You could see in her eyes that whatever she had done was not something she would forget. When it came to refugees, sometimes it was best to leave it at that. If someone talked, they might start crying. Opening wounds was always a painful process.

As Brath stared up at space, following Vardis' line of sight, he had to admit to himself he was curious to see the Dark One's face. Not that he took it lightly. But the curiosity was there. The face of the creature that was wiping out entire civilizations, a monster from another hellish dimension. Who wouldn't be a little curious?

Though it was much more than curiosity. Brath felt like he had to stare into the Dark One's face, to see what kind of madness really dwelled within that dark face. Would he be strong enough to look away, to hold on to his sanity? If he wasn't, was he strong enough to even be fighting in this war? If you couldn't look your enemy in the eye, were you even a warrior?

Alex screamed again, her pain ringing out in the darkness of space. Brath wished there was something to do, but Alex stopped screaming soon enough. Now she was only muttering in a fitful sleep. Brath hoped Jim would be able to concentrate on the fighting and ignore the state Alex was in. Humans were usually too emotional.

Brath knew Jim would be able to handle it, though. He'd watched the mech rider and Alex. They were strong. Resilient even by gnomish standards. Alex would be able to pull through. Brath had no doubt about it.

———

Jollies had found where she was going to camp out until the attack began. She'd located a small cluster of asteroids that were much larger than the rest. They would provide her with ample cover to avoid a direct attack. She was also practicing guiding Amber through the maze of asteroids.

If the situation hadn't been so dire, Jollies would have wanted to spend more time flying through the asteroids. Pushing herself and her dragon. Pushing her skills as a rider.

An unspoken secret of the Nest was what was often said about Jollies. She was one of the smallest riders, smaller than any of the other pixies, but she was easily the fastest. It took skill to ride that fast.

Speed wasn't something you just pushed yourself for. Speed took lightning-fast reflexes. It took the ability to process thousands of different things at once, and she and Amber worked together like a finely tuned precision engine. In action, they were a sight to behold, but that wasn't often seen. Most people couldn't track her. She was that fast.

Everything processed faster. Fear was usually the first to go, then worry, then back to fear, but faster than before. Always ending in anticipation.

The pixie didn't like to fight anything other than herself, and there was always something to be improved in her riding. She wouldn't be satisfied until it was perfect, and each battle was a test. Each victory honed her blade.

That was what she told herself, at least. The only alternative was to think about Alex, and she wasn't going to do that right now. That wouldn't help her. She knew Alex needed her right now, needed all of them, and that was that.

Once she started thinking, she was going to start feeling...and that was going to be distracting.

Her skin heated up as she fluctuated between colors in quick succession. Now that no one was around, she wasn't focused on maintaining her composure. Each emotion brought a new color. She let herself cycle through them, trying to focus and think about what was ahead.

She watched Brath pacing from afar, barely able to make him out. Hopefully she and Gill weren't too spread out. There had to be just the right amount of space for the vrosks to get thrown off. If they were too close, the vrosks would just come after them. But at *just* the right distance, the vrosks would have to choose between attacking her and Gill or descending and going after Brath and Jim.

Nothing can happen to Alex. I'll never get over it if she doesn't make it through this. Gods, her parents would be heartbroken. I'll be heartbroken. She's such a strong person, probably the strongest I've ever met, and she's made me a stronger person. Gods, this can't be happening. It's okay, I'll be there for her. We're all going to be. We can handle this.

Jollies' brain continued to rattle off worst-case scenarios as she tried to rein herself in a little bit. Not too much, though. Her emotions were her lifeblood. If she couldn't experience them, she was nothing. No pixie was. She'd simply die.

But she wasn't going to let those emotions get sloppy. Pixies learned a simple adage from a young age: *You are your feelings, and you are not your feelings.* It was a paradox all pixies lived by. Let them come and let them go.

She was going to cycle through them all again once the fight got started.

———

Gill was getting settled into his position. Timber's weapons were beginning to charge, and there was still some time before the Dark One's forces were going to begin their attack. This was where Gill felt the most comfortable—the calm before the storm.

The drow watched distant stars twinkling, their life force gone thousands and millions of years before he had existed. Even with a battle looming ahead of him, Gill could not ignore the vast beauty he was experiencing at this moment.

Few drow ever saw anything above the surface. They spent their lives underground, toiling for purposes that many of them weren't even certain of. It was the system Gill had been raised in. His parents had never seen the surface. Neither had his grandparents. He wasn't certain if anyone in his family ever had.

If Gill had been the kind of person to speak much, he would have gushed about how beautiful the blackness of space was, how close to the darkness he had grown up in it was. The infinite blackness seemed more like home than anything he'd ever seen in Middang3ard, and he was more than happy to enjoy these moments alone.

It was not that Gill didn't take the battle that awaited him seriously. He knew these might be his last living moments. But he also knew that was how every battle was and would be. Acknowledging that didn't mean he couldn't enjoy these small moments for what they were.

Beauty came in many forms; that was something he'd learned from his time underground, and even more so since he'd come above ground, out of the Underdark. Beauty was in the eye of the beholder. Some eyes had enough light to see certain things. Others were so blinded by that light that they couldn't see others.

Gill ran his hand over Timber's scales, soothing the dragon. They were both in a new environment, a place neither of them understood well. Not just the two of them, but all of Boundless was experiencing something completely outside their understanding.

As Gill pondered, he looked up and saw the massing of the vrosks above him. *Even their desire for destruction could be beautiful*, Gill thought. *In this darkness, even that could be beautiful.*

CHAPTER THREE

Jim was hauling Alex into his mech while Gill shouted that the battle was beginning. He didn't know what to do about Chine, but Brath was already moving Furi closer to defend the dragon. Hopefully, it wasn't going to come to that. Gill's and Brath's plan could work, but if it failed, they were all going to find out how terrible the Dark One was.

The back of Jim's mech popped open, and he placed Alex inside gently. She hardly stirred. Whatever the Dark One was doing to her was getting worse by the second. Jim wished there was something he could do, but he had no idea what was going on. The only way he could make himself helpful was by fighting. Maybe Alex would snap out of it by then.

Jim jumped into the mech and took a deep breath, pulling up his HUD, scanning for enemies and trying to figure out where they were going to come from. He had a bad case of nerves—something about having Alex in the cockpit with him. He wondered if she would feel the same way about him being on Chine's back with her.

He doubted his pre-battle ritual was going to bother her,

or if she was even going to notice. Jim hoped there was a signal out here in space. There had to be. He still had a comm link and updates from the Nest, so this wouldn't be a problem.

He looked over his shoulder at Alex again. She was still muttering under her breath in a language Jim couldn't quite put his finger on. It was extremely creepy and unsettling, and he was more worried for Alex than he'd ever been for anyone in his entire life. But that wasn't going to help. Getting his head in the game would.

Jim pulled up his playlist, aptly titled *The Best Funk and Disco the World has Ever Known*. He cranked up the volume, letting the choppy guitar cut in and out, the trumpets coming next as Diana Ross' voice came over the speakers, as clear as if Jim were listening to it live.

His right foot tapped along with the beat as he pulled on his seatbelt, checking again to see if Alex had registered the music. He had kinda been hoping the disco would pull her out of her state, but there was hardly any change. She was quieter than before.

Boogie Wonderland was the next song up. Jim could feel his shoulder twitch in time with the music. Anytime he put on this playlist, his body started to move on its own. It was the only thing he listened to when he flew, ever since he played VR. He used to leave one earbud under the headset.

Now it was second nature. If the mech was on, the funk was on. He'd even thought about getting a small disco ball when they had been on Earth.

All of those things seemed distant now. Childish to be worried about someone listening to him grooving while Alex was in the back of the mech fighting for her life. If she was watching him, she would probably be laughing her ass off.

Jim powered up the mech's thrusters. He wondered if he should have been up there among the asteroids instead of

Gill. The lack of gravity hadn't affected Jim's piloting skills at all. His mech had been designed to operate in space. It might have made more sense to have a rider who was able to move freely.

Planning had never been Jim's strength. When he and Alex used to play VR together, their idea of a plan was… vague at best, but somehow, they always got through it. Jim reminded himself of that right now. They always got through it.

As he was coaching himself through his thoughts, he saw the first indication that the vrosks were coming through. Gill was firing up ahead. Jim wasn't sure what he was shooting at. It must have been one of the weapons the dragons had been outfitted with to make up for their lack of flames.

Then he saw the vrosks, more than Boundless had anticipated. Enough to make him take a deep breath and think they were going to need a better plan. But then the funk came back to him.

Two cylindrical tubes came out from the middle of the cockpit, which were coated with a cold gel. Jim plunged his hands into the tubes, his suit connecting his nerves to the mech, allowing him a great deal of control.

Another reason Jim was nervous about Alex seeing him pilot his mech was that things were going to look a little bit weird.

Jim leaned forward as two more tubes pushed up from the bottom of the cockpit, connecting his legs to the mech.

This was the way the newer models worked. Total body immersion was the eventual goal. The mechs were always being updated with new neural networks and a host of other things Jim was not really able to understand.

What he did understand was the feeling of piloting. Every iteration made the distinction between man and machine slimmer. Jim wouldn't be surprised if eventually, he wasn't able to tell where the mech began and ended.

The neural link went live and Jim pressed his face to his HUD that wrapped around his face, letting him see as if he were actually looking out of the mech. *And now for the weird part*, Jim thought as the back neural transmitter came out from Jim's chair—a wide, sponge-like pad covered in a slimy, sticky substance that sparked when it attached itself to the back of Jim's neck.

Now he was completely connected.

Jim turned the mech's head up to get a better look at the vrosks that were pouring into the asteroid field. Gill was lighting them up from above, and Jim could see Jollies flying in and out of the pack. Bodies were starting to fall. "Maybe we can do this," Jim muttered to himself.

Brath was at Jim's side, getting ready to start their part of the plan. Jim was glad it was Brath down here with him. Furi had some major firepower in the form of his flames and, even though that wasn't an option, Brath had loaded equivalent augments.

Some of the vrosks started to try to move away from the area Gill was firing from. They went straight down, just like the Boundless had assumed they were going to.

Jim lined up his first shot. He wanted to start this off with a bang, letting those vrosks know he meant business. His machine gun had been practically useless against the kin, and he didn't want to risk the same thing here.

A gun-lance swung out of Jim's mech's side, a long rifle-like weapon that used an extremely powerful plasma-charged blast for pinpoint accuracy.

Jim took aim at a vrosk and fired.

The gun-lance heated up, charged the bolt, and then fired. The shot tore through the vrosks, taking at least three down as it found its intended target. Then the bolt exploded, sending plasma flying at the vrosks unlucky enough to be nearby.

Jim lined up another shot as a group of vrosks started downward at the asteroid Brath and Jim were on. He fired again, splitting up the group of vrosks, but they quickly regrouped and continued closing in for the attack.

At Jim's side, Furi stood up on his hind legs. The cannons on the dragon's shoulder pulled back, and what looked like two steel dragon claws took their place. The claws started to glow, a ring of pure energy forming on each of them, spinning until they flew toward at the vrosks. They cut through body after body until they returned to Brath like boomerangs.

Jim laughed. He wouldn't have thought Brath would choose something so creative.

There were still way too many vrosks heading toward Jim and Brath. He decided the herd needed to be thinned, so he stood up in his mech and hit his thrusters and flew at the vrosks. He pulled in his lance-gun and heated up his energy claws.

There were a lot of vrosks, but it didn't look like they felt comfortable flying in space. Some of them were wielding magical staffs, others had plasmas rifles. The rifles didn't concern Jim very much. The plasma blasts operated the same in space as they would anywhere else. The magical staffs were a whole other question.

One of the vrosks prepared to answer that very question. As it got closer, its staff began to glow bright red, and it launched a fireball at his mech.

Jim banked hard to the left, giving himself enough room to avoid the blast as he slammed into another vrosk. He drove his claws through its chest before hitting another with his sharpened wings, tearing it in half before firing his machine gun.

At this range, the machine gun was capable of doing real damage. As the vrosks tried to get their bearings, Jim took advantage of his superior flying ability. He whipped around the group, putting a good distance between them before lowering his gun lance again. He was close enough that he didn't have to aim. He charged it and fired two blasts.

The blasts ripped through the vrosks as Jim headed back toward where Brath was. Two of Brath's energy rings whisked past him, slicing through those that were attempting to follow the mech. "Thanks for that!" Jim sent over the comm.

Brath gave him a thumbs-up as Furi launched a gravity well. His well worked differently than Chine's. Rather than pulling everyone toward it, it did the opposite—shot out a gravitational field that pushed everything away in a giant explosion.

The result was that vrosks went flying away from the well as Brath's energy rings zoomed around the battlefield, cutting through anything they got close to.

As Jim touched down, he called to Jollies, "Hey, how are you guys doing up there?"

The pixie replied, "There are a ton of these things, but I think we're past the first volley. Gill said he can see more coming through. He thinks they're coming in waves. Probably trying to tire us out."

Above the mech, Jollies flew between a cluster of vrosks, dropping small electrical proximity mines as she went. She headed toward the blank space the vrosks had come from and lined the break in the asteroids with the same mines.

Jim's tactical map updated, showing him where the mines were so he could avoid them.

From the back of the mech, Alex muttered, "Funnel them toward the mines. Front and back."

Jim turned to see Alex sitting up, rubbing her head as she

looked at the tactical display. "Holy crap, you're okay!" he gasped.

Alex still looked ready to pass out. "I sure as hell don't feel okay," she muttered. "Also, you look ridiculous. Oh, and good music choice. The seventies never died, baby."

Jim didn't have time to be embarrassed and repeated what Alex had said to Jollies. Then he turned back to the rider and asked, "You're not thinking about getting out there, are you?"

Alex shook her head as she leaned against the back of the mech. "There's no way I could," she answered. "I've been in and out. Like, I see what's going on, but the Dark One is in my head. Kind of. Not like the telepathy Chine uses. This is different. He's not reading my mind or anything. It's more like he's filling it. With himself."

"Like back at the meteor."

"Exactly. I just got back in contact with Chine, and he said it's going to wear off soon. He's already a lot better, but I'm going to need a minute."

Above, the first wave of vrosks had been completely decimated. "Not to rush you, but you might have to hurry up. The next wave is coming soon, and we could use the extra firepower."

Alex laughed before wincing in pain. "Really? Looks like you guys got everything covered. I might even be able to take a break."

A huge explosion went off above Brath, Jim, and Alex. Another portal was opening near the barer side of the asteroid field. "Or not," Alex muttered.

CHAPTER FOUR

This new portal was no different than the one that had brought the Dark One into her world. But it wasn't vrosks coming through the portal this time. Ships very similar to the long-tendrilled thing that had appeared from the other portal were coming through. They weren't nearly as long, and they didn't have the hulking mass of tendrils, but they also seemed to be made from flesh, much like the Dark One's ship.

The Dark One's voice had subsided from Alex's mind. She still wasn't sure what she had been listening to. It was obvious it was his voice. She'd heard it before. But this time it was different. Not as concise. Almost rambling. His feelings. Fear.

Alex didn't have the time to try to understand what the Dark One was afraid of. Obviously, it wasn't the dragonriders. Not the four of them, at least. Maybe it was what they were trying to bring back. The weapon Vardis had promised.

The Dark One's warning hung over Alex's head, though. His warning of what Vardis' weapon would actually do. This could easily have been a ploy. How did you trust someone who enslaved entire races? Mind games were assumed.

Alex was still getting used to being back in her body. She didn't know where she had been before, but it was definitely not where she was now. Talking to Myrddin about what she experienced would be helpful. Hopefully, he'd be able to give her some kind of guidance.

But for now, there was a fleet of ships coming through a portal from another dimension, along with a horde of vrosks and two interdimensional beings, and it was obvious which one was trying to destroy reality.

Alex sat up in the back of the mech. "You need to let me out of here."

Jim pulled his arms and head out of the neural connection, his eyes confused and wide. "Are you serious? You just woke up. You're in no position to—"

"We need everyone on deck. You see what we're up against. If I'm okay, Chine has to be too. We're getting sky-ready. Let me out."

Jim didn't argue any further. He hit the lever for his cockpit, and it popped open.

Alex climbed out and said, "Thanks for taking care of me. And I'm not forgetting about the disco jams. Ever." She leaped down and headed toward Chine, reaching out to him mentally.

Chine answered quickly enough, even if he sounded groggy. *I assume we're going to be joining the fight.*

Alex ran over to Chine and leaped onto his back, looking at his scars and burns. *I talked a big game, but if you can't fight, we're going to sit this one out.*

Chine looked at the wounds on his arms and sighed heavily. *I'll live. But...*

Alex didn't need to be told twice. She plunged her dragon

anchor into Chine's spine, drawing out the draconic fluid that was no doubt burning through his skin.

As that was going on, she felt a wave of heat passing over her body. That had happened a few times since she'd absorbed the fluid into her anchor, but this time it was different. It didn't hurt nearly as much. It was almost comforting. She looked down at her anchor, and the readings said she'd absorbed enough so that Chine wouldn't be in any pain. "Let's do this," she said.

Alex pulled up on her anchor, feeling like she had more control over Chine than during the last battle they had been in. Maybe he was relaxing. Maybe she just had a better idea of what she was doing. It didn't matter; the connection was there. *It could be the binding,* Alex thought, still very aware she didn't understand what the binding really meant.

You didn't have to know the details about something to know it worked, though. Alex's dad could drive a car. Didn't mean he knew anything about combustion. With that, Alex soared into the blackness of space. "Boundless, thanks for holding it down for me while I was out," she shouted. "Let me know what's going on."

If any of her team was surprised by her being back on the battlefield, they didn't let her know. Gill answered before anyone else. "We've been trying to funnel the vrosks down to Furi and Jim since they have the most firepower, but we weren't prepared for the influx of forces. We could stick with the original plan, but it doesn't take into account what the ships can do."

Alex was watching the ships. They were small enough to be fighters, which made the most sense. That meant that they were going to be fast and mobile. The Dark One's flagship was probably packing a lot of heat, but it couldn't maneuver through the asteroid field. That was why it was hanging back.

Options were weighed quickly. "Jollies, I want you with me. Gill, keep doing what you can to get them to move toward Jim and Brath. We have enough firepower to deal with these guys. We just have to make sure we aren't overwhelmed. If we keep our distance and spread them out like you were doing, we should be able to handle this."

Brath interrupted Alex's train of thought. His voice was surprisingly unnerved. "What about the Dark One's ship?"

"We'll worry about that when we have to."

Alex scanned for Vardis, who turned around and met her eyes. His thoughts came through to her. *I will be joining this battle as well.*

Why the hell hadn't he joined it before? Alex thought. *Glad to hear you'll be joining us,* she sent, trying to keep her tone even.

"What should I do?"

From where Alex was standing, it didn't seem like Vardis was capable of doing much. He hadn't helped with the kin. All she had seen him do was fly and use his telepathy. "Whatever you can," she finally told him. "But don't endanger the weapon. I'd rather have you make it back to Earth with it than fight now."

Vardis' face hardened. "Nothing will happen to the weapon."

"I'm going to hold you to that. If you're going to help now, I'll leave it at that."

The portal above had finally closed. Whatever reinforcements the Dark One had sent for were here. Nothing else was coming through for the time being. Alex wondered if that was the extent of what the Dark One had at the moment. Maybe that was why he was so reliant on personnel from the other races of the nine realms.

Alex sped toward the fighter ships that had come through the portal. In her peripheral vision, she noticed Vardis leaping onto one of the asteroids. He wasn't flying as he had done before, and it didn't seem like the lack of gravity meant anything to him. He bounded from one asteroid to the next.

The asteroids posed a slight problem, but one Alex felt she was able to handle. She wove through them as she approached the bulk of vrosks, who had massed where the portal had closed. Gill shot out of his hiding place, heading toward her.

Three of the vrosks veered off from the rest. They were coming for Alex, but she wasn't going to let them be the ones who brought the party.

Alex leaned forward with her anchor, driving Chine toward them as Gill came up on her side. "We can bust through and scatter them," she suggested.

Chine fired a small explosive gravity attack, similar to a proximity mine. That reminded Alex of what she'd heard the team planning earlier. "Wait, Jollies already prepped for this!" she shouted.

Alex pulled up her tactical display and saw where Jollies had dropped the mines. "All right, we're funneling them that way!"

Alex shot a small gravitational well ahead of the vrosks who were coming toward them. It exploded, pulling them in but fizzling out enough to give the vrosks the impression that they weren't going to affect it too heavily.

The vrosks took the bait, along with all the others behind them. They flew after Alex and Gill, who headed toward the mines the vrosks had managed to miss by coming through their portal.

While Alex and Gill were handling the enemies in front of them, Jim and Brath were continuing to fire their artillery, taking care of the vrosks who had forgotten about them. They didn't bother with the ships.

Vardis was standing on the edge of one of the asteroids, looking at the ships that had come through the portal.

Suddenly, he let out a scream of rage, and an aura of golden fire surrounded him. He leaped toward one of the ships, landing on top of it.

The ship veered to the left, trying to shake Vardis, who held on regardless of the speed. Vardis raised his right hand, and it began glowing with energy. He gathered a ball of it in his hand and slammed it into the ship's hull as the tendrils tried to wrap around him.

Vardis tore through the hull and grabbed the pilot, an orc whose skin seemed to be rotting off the bone. He flung him into the coldness of space.

The orc clasped his throat, trying to breathe, but quickly succumbed to the vacuum of space. His body drifted out into the darkness as Vardis leaped to the next ship. It barrel-rolled, trying to throw the alien off but failing miserably. Vardis pierced the hull with his hand again, this time causing the whole ship to explode as he leaped through the flames toward the next.

Alex watched the carnage Vardis was unleashing on the Dark One's forces. To say she was surprised would have been an understatement. There was no way she could have known that Vardis was packing so much power.

Or rage. It was almost tangible, the anger and hatred coming off Vardis. It was so strong that both the vrosks and the dragonriders stopped for a second, watching the seething destruction Vardis deemed proper for the forces of the Dark One.

Alex took the chance to implement the second part of her plan. Jollies had done more than just set up mines around the initial perimeters. She'd set mines up on the other side of the asteroid belt as well. Alex fired two laser beams at the vrosks in front of her, catching them off-guard. Then she and Gill sped toward the last line of mines, swooping low to give Jim and Furi a chance to pick off any vrosks they could.

They fired a flurry of specially made space grenades that exploded on contact, and a weapon Brath was just unveiling now. Furi stood up on his hind legs, showing what looked like a harness across his chest. But the harness had a bulge in the middle, resting on his sternum.

The dragon roared loudly, and the bulge, which was molten metal, shot out at a remarkable speed and formed into multiple different projectiles. They maintained the same speed and density and tore through vrosks flying overhead.

The horde of vrosks had been noticeably thinned, and the rest were following Alex and Gill closely, firing their magical staffs. Alex and Gill wove in and out of the asteroids as Jollies showed up to provide backup, flying between the vrosks and electrocuting whichever wasn't paying close enough attention.

Finally, Alex and Gill got to the mines. They swooped down into them and turned around to make themselves seem like better targets. Just in case the vrosks didn't take the bait, Alex prepped another gravitational well and tossed it out.

The vrosks were already heading in, though. The gravity well went off and the vrosks were pulled toward the mines, which instantly detonated as Boundless flew out of the blast's proximity.

They headed back toward Brath and Jim, who were prepping for the next wave of enemies. Vardis was still leaping from ship to ship. They couldn't avoid him, no matter how fast they were.

The team sat down on the asteroid together and watched Vardis working. "Didn't know he had it in him," Jim muttered. "Didn't seem like much of a fighter."

Alex was watching the place the portal had opened. "No, I wouldn't have thought so. We can't do this all day, though. If the Dark One opens portal after portal, we're gonna get tired. We need to retreat."

No one disagreed. They had probably all been waiting to hear those words.

"We're gonna move now before they send more rein-forcements. Get the hell out of here while we still can."

The plan was straightforward enough. There seemed to be a lag before another portal could open, and they were going to take advantage of that and hoof it straight back to the base. She was uncertain about whether the Dark One would give chase.

Brath thought it was a terrible idea. "You guys will end up like the gnome world. Maybe even worse. The Dark One never landed on our planet. Can you imagine the damage he could do?"

"I don't think so. Look at this whole fight. If the Dark One was powerful enough to wipe us out single-handedly, he wouldn't have brought a small army with him. He might be strong, but he's not a god, no matter what he keeps trying to tell me. He needs forces, and he obviously doesn't have enough to deal with us. He won't have enough to deal with the base on Earth."

Brath had nothing to say back to that, and neither did the rest of Boundless. Alex did have a point. If the Dark One could just kill everything, why would he bother with armies? Unless he was after something else.

Alex thought back to what she'd heard the Dark One saying. The weapon Vardis had was strong enough to destroy life as she knew it.

And the Dark One didn't want that. He wanted things to keep living.

"He won't do it," Alex said finally. "He's not here to destroy."

Jim opened his cockpit and leaned out. "I know you've spent a little time in the Dark One's head, but I don't think you should start taking his thoughts as the Lord's truth. We can't trust him, not even what his mind tells you. He might just be trying to manipulate us."

Alex knew Jim was partially right. She couldn't believe any thoughts she'd received from the Dark One, but she *could* make use of the connection between the two of them.

Jollies was flapping her wings anxiously while Amber huffed out a small storm of electricity. "Are we going to sit around and talk about retreating, or are we going to wait until we have a big enough group of vrosks to retreat from? I think if we're going to go, now is probably the best chance we have."

As Jollies was speaking, the portal opened again. The Dark One's tendrilled ship came through first, with more ships and vrosks following him. Alex felt the familiar dread creep over her at the sight of the ship. She knew the rest of Boundless was feeling it as well.

Vardis, who had just rejoined them, was the only one who didn't seem to be affected by the sight of the flagship, or at least not like the rest of the Boundless. He looked livid, as if it was impossible for him to hold his anger inside.

She still didn't know what to make of the alien. He obviously hated the Dark One, but he'd been less than forthright about many things, and the situation with the kin had almost seemed like a backhanded attack. But why would he have attacked them while they were helping him get something he wanted? There was no motive.

From where Alex stood, Vardis was just as trustworthy as the Dark One. *Hey, Chine,* Alex thought, *do you think you could help me reach the Dark One? The way that he reaches out to me?*

The dragon's voice sounded proud when he responded. *I don't think you'll need my help. I've been watching your telepathic abilities grow. You might not realize it, but you've been doing most of the heavy lifting recently.*

Do you think it's safe?

I don't think seeking a conversation with him is in any way safe, but I don't think you need my protection. I will listen in, though.

Alex turned to the rest of Boundless. "We're not retreating yet. You guys can deal with another wave, right?"

Brath yawned as he drew his axe and leaned on it. "I got another four in me. What about you, Gill?"

Gill, who was sitting cross-legged, stood and stretched his arms and legs. "At least three at the current number of troops and resting times between the portal's opening. Jollies?"

"Five. I'm not using nearly as much energy as you guys. Jim?"

"I think I might need to gas up after four or five, but that's my only concern."

Alex folded her arms and nodded, satisfied with her team's answers. "Good. Chine's going to watch my back. I'm going to have a talk with the Dark One and try to come to some kind of agreement. The way I see it, we have a weapon that can instantly kill him. He might not know we know how to use it."

Vardis' eyes widened as he turned to face Alex, his whole body shaking with what could only have been rage. "You can't be serious. You're going to talk to him?"

Alex didn't bother to meet Vardis' eyes. She was looking at the Dark One's ship. "I think it's about time we had a talk on my terms."

CHAPTER FIVE

I t felt like second nature. First reaching inward, finding her voice. The voice she'd been using all along when she spoke with Chine. The voice Myrddin and Vardis had both drawn out of her. The voice the Dark One had tried to drown out when she'd found herself within his mind. The voice was there. It was strong—stronger than she'd been aware of.

Alex wondered how long the voice had been there. There had never been any occasion for her to use anything like telepathy. She assumed the way she'd moved around the world when she was blind was because she'd grown used to it.

But if she thought, really thought back, she could remember instances of strong feelings and picking up on things people felt even though she couldn't see their reactions or body language. It was a deep knowing as if she was somehow connected to them.

Those feelings had grown since she'd been bound to her dragon. It wasn't something she would have put into words before, but for some reason, everything was clicking now.

Chine had sharpened her telepathy by proximity and communication. She wondered if that was how it was for the rest of the dragonriders, but it was doubtful. If it had been like that, they would have talked about it by now, having sensed it growing in each of them.

Above, the vrosks and fighter ships were preparing to attack. Boundless was gearing up to go on the defensive and turn the tide. They all seemed fairly certain that they were going to be able to handle whatever the Dark One was throwing at them, and there was no lack of trust in Alex and what she was capable of.

Alex took a seat next to her dragon, who covered her with his wing, promising to keep her safe. *I appreciate it*, Alex said. *I don't know what's going to happen when I get in there.*

Chine chuckled softly as he flexed his wing. *If it's anything like last time, it will be somewhat terrifying.*

Somewhat? That's an understatement. Alex called to Brath, "Hey, little guy. You're in command while I'm out, okay?"

Brath puffed up his chest as Furi reared. "What the hell do you mean, 'little guy'?"

"I was talking to Furi."

Brath fake-laughed as Furi stamped the ground. "Hurry up," Brath chided. "We could use the extra firepower."

As Alex was preparing to telepathically call out to the Dark One, Vardis walked over to her, crouching to her eye level. It was the first time Alex had noticed how physically imposing the alien was. When they'd been back at the Nest, he'd looked frail behind the glass walls. Now, out here, Alex could see how strong he really was. His attack on the fighter jets hadn't hurt that impression either.

Vardis peered at Alex, his deep, dark eyes difficult to read. "This is a foolish idea. The Dark One has broken people with his mind. He is not—"

Alex didn't have time to waste talking to Vardis, especially if he was going to try to talk her out of something her mind was already made up about. "I've been in there before, and I came out alive. During the last psychic attack, he hit me with something I could live through as well. I advise you to keep up with everyone else."

Vardis' inner eye flickered as he leaned back on his haunches. "If you wish. Be safe."

"You too."

Vardis stood and stalked off as Alex tried to relax. She closed her eyes and found the voice in her again. Once she found it, she turned it outward, projecting it toward the Dark One's ship. But that wasn't quite right. She was imagining the ship and a physical body to connect with, yet the more she thought about the Dark One, the more her imagination warped and changed until she realized she was looking for a voice. One she'd already spoken to.

Boundless took off to confront the vrosks and ships above. Alex could hear explosions going off. She could see them, yet at the same time, they were blending together and peeling apart. It was as if someone had thrown water on an oil painting and was rubbing it clean.

Then it all broke apart like a stained glass mirror hit with a rock. The darkness of space receded like a wave, and what was beneath it was much deeper darkness. Alex looked down at her feet. She could see Boundless and Vardis engaging the enemy.

Alex felt a vibration course through her head like an earthquake. She was tumbling, trying to grasp something to keep from slipping through the cracks. Insanity lay down there. She didn't need to have it explained to her.

The vibration subsided. Alex felt something stirring in her for a second, then it shot out like a white light, cutting through the darkness and illuminating something at the far end of infinity. "What do you want, human?" the Dark One thundered.

The light receded, coming back to Alex like it was on a string. "You know my name. Don't act like you don't."

"Alex."

"Why haven't you killed us? If you're strong enough to wipe out entire universes, what are you doing playing with a bunch of teenagers on flying lizards?"

Something like a laugh emerged, and Alex was surprised that it didn't sound malicious. The darkness grew even darker. "You have something I want, something I need. Today, we have the same goal: to keep existence from ending."

"How do you know the weapon is going to do that?"

Another laugh, this one drenching everything in sludgy darkness. "I have seen its effect. It will wipe out all living matter on this plane."

Alex focused again, sending out another beam of light, dispelling a little bit of darkness. She could see an uncount-able number of black hands drawing back. "How do I know I can trust you?"

"Look down."

Alex glanced at the fight taking place below. A black wave of energy formed around the Dark One's flagship. Without warning, the energy took the shape of a crescent and snapped across the battlefield, cutting through ships, vrosks, and nearly Jim, who wasn't able to pull away. The attack stopped at Jim's mech's face.

The Dark One laughed again, and black hands clawed at Alex. "If I wanted you dead, you would be. But that is not why I am here. I will bend this universe to my will and remake it in my image. What cannot withstand the fires of my purification will be turned to ash and abandoned. You, though… You could live through the fires. And I promise you this."

The darkness peeled back, showing a bony black hand dripping red and black ooze into a golden goblet. "I offer you this pact: fight beside me. I will give you an army. Fight under my wing, and I will give you the strength you've dreamt of."

Alex could have laughed at the offer, but she didn't, and she didn't know why. Something in her heard the Dark One and wanted to hear more. She was certain it wasn't due to any influence from the Dark One's mind. Deep down, she wanted more.

Instead of answering, Alex looked at the battle raging beneath her.

Jim had landed on an asteroid and was hanging off, firing missile after missile at the vrosks who were attempting to swarm him.

Across from him, Gill had swooped in to provide backup. He fired a gravitational well, and Jollies infused it with electricity that electrocuted anything that was pulled into it.

The Dark One's voice oozed through the cracks in Alex's brain. "They would be generals in your army. An entire realm to rule. It could be yours. Just give me the weapon."

Beneath Alex, Brath was flying through space, Furi ripping vrosks in half as ships fired at the dragon. He barrel-rolled and blocked the attack with his wings.

"Give. Me. *THE WEAPON!*"

It was not a shout, merely a thought that grew stronger with each word.

Alex wasn't going to give in. Whatever the Dark One offered, she didn't want any of it. "No deal. I don't give a crap about being one of your servants. But the weapon…how do I know you aren't lying?"

"You saw how easily I could destroy you all. I'll retreat.

Take it as a sign of good faith. I don't need the weapon. Keep it. Destroy it. It matters not to me. All that matters is that Vardis not be allowed to use it."

Alex weighed her options. "Withdraw your troops. We'll keep in touch."

Alex snapped out of the trance, nearly falling over. Chine caught her and helped her to her feet.

A portal had opened in the blackness of space. The Dark One's forces headed through it. Finally, all that was left was the flagship. It hung back as if it were watching the dragonriders. Then it turned and flew through the portal as well. There was a bright flash, and the portal closed.

Boundless and Vardis flew down to the asteroid Alex and her dragon were on. "What the hell was that all about?" Jim asked. "Did they just retreat?"

Gill leaped off his dragon, smiling widely. "Either Alex is extremely mentally intimidating, or she single-handedly brokered a peace treaty with the Dark One."

Alex shook her head as she stared at Earth. "Hardly. I don't know why he left. Maybe I'm just a bad conversationalist."

The members of Boundless chuckled, although some of them cast dubious glances in Alex's direction, which she mitigated with a genuine smile.

Vardis, on the other hand, did not seem satisfied by Alex's answer. Alex couldn't read the alien's body language, but she gleaned enough from his mind. He was sulking. Whatever he assumed had happened between Alex and the Dark One had upset him.

That was enough to keep her suspicious.

CHAPTER SIX

Boundless arrived back at the base within the hour. They wasted no time entering the atmosphere after their battle with the Dark One. No one had talked during the entire ride back. Alex was glad. She didn't want to have to explain the conversation she'd had with the Dark One to the rest of the team while Vardis was near.

Nor did Alex want to address how what the Dark One had said affected her. She had been strongly interested in his promises of power, and she still wasn't sure if that desire had come from her or the Dark One's manipulations. If he was such a strong telepath, could he use mind control without her realizing it?

That train of thought made Alex feel like she was trying to run away from the truth. She knew the Dark One used technology to control the minds of his victims. By now, that was common knowledge in the war for Middang3ard.

But the truth didn't rest easy in Alex's mind: she had wanted the power the Dark One had promised.

When the dragonriders landed at the base, they were taken to the debriefing room. When the soldiers came to

38

escort Alex and the rest of the riders to their debriefing, Vardis stepped between them. "No," he said, "We need to talk."

Alex could see no traces of emotion in Vardis' eyes, but she caught everything in his mind. It wasn't quite anger; that was too vague. The closest comparison was the time her parents had accused her of sneaking desserts from the fridge and punished her, only to find out later that her father had forgotten he'd eaten them all.

Anger mixed with betrayal mixed with mistrust. Alex had no idea what Vardis had to mistrust. The riders had done exactly what they said they were going to do: escort him to pick up the weapon and bring it back to Earth. The only thing Alex could think of was that Vardis wasn't happy about the conversation she'd had with the Dark One.

Then Vardis opened his mouth and proved her right. "Do your commanding officers know you spoke directly to the Dark One? To one of the most powerful psychics in all the realms?"

Alex tried to meet Vardis' gaze with as much indifference as his eyes betrayed while focusing on her emotions, making sure they weren't broadcasting as strongly as Vardis' were. "My commanding officers are about to find out that I did because I'll tell them, just like I did the rest of you. I don't have any secrets from them. Do you?"

Vardis' emotions shut down; he was like a closed book now. "I've been nothing but straightforward with all of you. I hope the mishap on the moon won't tarnish our working relationship in the future."

Jim and Gill had already walked away, but Alex could hear Brath muttering under his breath. "Mishap? Is that what he's calling nearly getting us all killed?"

Jollies said, "Everyone makes mistakes. And he said someone hacked into his defense program."

Couldn't be that well-hidden if someone found it before us, Alex thought. *And if they could hack into the system, why didn't they just take the weapon?*

Alex put on her best fake smile, which was terrible because she hadn't quite gotten the hang of lying to someone's face. "I'll find you after we finish our briefing. They're probably going to want to hold onto that shard in the meantime."

Vardis nodded his assent as he bowed. "It only makes sense."

Alex walked away, joining the rest of Boundless as a soldier approached Vardis and guided him to another part of the base. She jogged to catch up with the soldier leading them and asked, "Would it be possible to do the debrief in the stables? Our dragons have been through a lot, and we should really take care of them first."

The soldier agreed to the request and told Alex he would make the arrangements. As he and the other soldier walked off, Alex and the rest of Boundless headed toward the stables.

Alex looked over her shoulder to make sure they had left. "There was another reason I asked for a change of meeting. I needed a moment to talk to you guys away from anyone else."

Jollies clapped her hands and flew to Alex's shoulder. "Secrets! My favorite."

"Not a secret. I'm going to let them know in the briefing. I wanted you to hear it from me first, though. When I was talking with the Dark One, he said he could make me a general. If we handed over the weapon, he said all of us would be able to rule our own realms."

Gill stopped walking and eyed Alex. "He offered you a deal?"

"It was weird. At first, I thought he wanted the weapon,

but he eventually said he would consider us destroying the weapon the same as giving it to him. He just wants it gone."

Jim pointed toward the stable, still walking. "We should keep moving. Don't want anyone to start staring. I'm assuming you told him we'd sign up as soon as possible, right?"

The rest of Boundless burst out laughing. Alex was glad that was how they responded. She'd been worried they'd be suspicious of her.

Now that Alex felt more comfortable, she went into the details. "The whole thing was weird. He seemed to really want to impress on me that he could have killed us any time he wanted and that I could trust him. He said Vardis couldn't be trusted. Didn't say why, though."

Brath grunted and leaned his head back as if the whole conversation was getting on his nerves. "Great. Now the guy we're trying to kill is messing with our heads. This is above our pay grade. Wait, do we even get paid?"

The members of Boundless looked at each other. "Hey, that's a good question," Jim said. "Soldiers get paid. Shouldn't we?"

Gill was the only member of Boundless who looked nonplussed. "Of course we get paid. Each of us has our own account. You can access them through your HUD. But I think there are more important things to be talking about now. What did you tell him, Alex?"

Alex shrugged as they neared the stables. "I told him I wasn't joining his army, and that I'd keep in touch. Don't know how yet, though. It's not like I have him on speed dial. I didn't give him any more information. Like I said, I wanted you guys to hear it from me before anyone else."

Jim put his hand on Alex's shoulder. "Thanks. I appreciate it. I'm assuming everyone else does as well."

There was no disagreement, although Brath still looked

annoyed at having to have the conversation to begin with. Alex could see why. Brath hated the Dark One more than anyone else in Boundless, and with good reason.

They entered the stables and got to work draining their dragons. It was slow, gruesome work. There was a lot more than usual. The gear that had been made for their space travel had been better than a prototype, but there were obviously kinks to be worked out.

None of the dragons were talkative, Chine in particular. They roared and groaned as their riders detached the armor and augments that had been placed on them.

About halfway through, soldiers came in with holoscreens to project their conversation with Myrddin. Alex didn't waste any time explaining the situation to Myrddin, talking as she took care of her dragon, occasionally stopping or wincing from the searing pain in her arms.

Myrddin promised he'd be at the base in a few hours and thanked them for their efforts in the war. Typical businesslike wizard.

Once the briefing was over, the soldiers excused themselves and the riders continued their maintenance. Chine's took the longest since his body was covered in burns from the explosion he and Alex had caused.

Alex put in a requisition with the Nest for ointments and salves for him and asked them to send a healer if they could spare one. Then she called Abby.

Abby picked up after a few rings. "Hey, what's up? Wasn't expecting to hear back from you for a bit."

"Hey," Alex said awkwardly. "I just… I was wondering if you had any more information about the shard I sent you?"

Abby took a second to answer. Alex thought she could hear the disappointment in the girl's voice. "Oh. Well, actually, no. We are still looking into it. Is that all you—"

"Actually, I wanted to know if you wanted to hang out

with the team next time you can get some leave. Figured you're probably getting tired of hanging out at the old folks' home."

"Yeah! That would be great. I can get a few days off soon. I'll message you, okay?"

"Sounds good. I'll talk to you later."

"Gotcha. Stay safe."

Abby hung up, and Alex sighed. She was glad she'd said why she meant to call. It was hard enough to make friends. Even harder to let someone know you wanted to be friends.

When Alex looked around the stables, they were empty. Chine was sleeping, as were the rest of the dragons. Maybe it was time for her to get some sleep too.

***

Alex was outside the barracks, looking at the stars. She and Jollies were bunking in one that was currently unused. Jollies had already gone to sleep. Alex couldn't sleep, though. She could only watch the stars.

During the mission, before everything had turned into an utter crap show, Alex had recorded some footage to send to her dad. She pulled up her HUD and watched the videos. They were breathtaking.

Alex wondered how there could be so much beauty in the universe, and the only reason she was seeing any of it was because of this damn war. If it weren't for the Dark One, she'd still be blind.

That thought made Alex sick to her stomach. She felt like in some perverse way, she owed her sight to the Dark One. It wasn't like she'd done anything to earn it. She'd just been good at a video game—one that only existed because of the Dark One.

Something moved in the darkness and Alex was on her feet, scythe drawn. "Who's there?"

Vardis stepped out of the shadows. "The feeling doesn't go away, you know," he whispered.

Alex's lip curled without her even thinking about it. "What are you talking about?"

"Owing him. For making your life anything but unremarkable."

Alex felt like kicking herself. She should have known to guard her thoughts. To be fair, though, she wasn't certain what guarding her thoughts would look like. "I'm assuming you can relate?"

Vardis didn't walk much farther out from the shadows. "For some of us, there was no life before our war with the Dark One."

Hatred, pure and hot, radiated from Vardis as he spoke. "Some of us were born into violence, into this...constant battle for existence. We would be nothing without the Dark One. What would my life be if I had grown up on a world like this with a family that loved me? If I had been given the luxury of hope?"

The hate coming off Vardis was hitting Alex like a wave of heat. It was almost enough to suffocate her. She tried to push back against it, but she had nothing to counter Vardis' feelings. All she could do was make sure she wasn't overrun by them. "I don't owe him anything," Alex said. "I don't owe anyone anything."

"Is that so? Myrddin? Your parents? None of them?"

Alex shook her head as she folded her arms. "I didn't ask for help. Didn't ask to be born. They gave what they wanted, and I worked for what I got. Yeah, I got help. That's not the same as being in someone's debt."

Vardis looked toward the stars as if he'd grown bored

with the conversation. "That's an interesting way to look at things. What did you and the Dark One discuss?"

"You know, just catching up and—"

Before Alex could finish speaking, she felt the air around her heat up. Vardis was in front of her, nearly nose to nose. She screamed and stumbled back, feeling more than just hatred coming off the alien. Pure energy was radiating from him as if he were merely a vessel for some intense power.

Alex scrambled to her feet and stood glaring into Vardis' dark eyes, which never stopped watching her. "What the hell—"

Vardis raised his hand, silencing Alex. "Do not lie to me, human."

Anger flashed across Alex's face, and her skin unexpectedly burst into flames, the draconic energy activating in her.

Vardis stepped back, caught off-guard by Alex resisting his intimidation.

The flames quickly burned out, but the fire was still in Alex's eyes. "I don't report to you," Alex growled. "I suggest you go back to your room."

The negative emotions and energy coming off Vardis vanished, and he ceased looking like a threat. Now it was hard for Alex to see him as anything other than a nuisance. "Apologies if I've kept you too long," he said as he bowed slightly and disappeared into the night.

Alex stayed outside for a little longer, watching where Vardis had gone. She didn't trust him, but she had no idea what kind of game he was playing. Even worse, it seemed like the most trustworthy person at this moment was the Dark One. "God, I hope this crap gets easier."

CHAPTER SEVEN

The next two days were given to team Boundless to recoup from the mission. Each member of the team found that when they woke up the next day, they were hardly able to get out of bed. Jim was the first to call the medics in due to him being the first to rise.

By the time Alex woke up, medics were stationed around her bed. Apparently, no one at the base had taken into account how much wear and tear was put on the rider's bodies by flying *and* fighting in space.

Myrddin showed up to speak with Alex privately after she'd been released from her medical check. He was waiting for her in her barracks, sipping a cup of tea while the medics brought her in, sitting in a wheelchair. "Glad to see you're still walking. No pun intended."

The medics helped Alex get into bed and propped her up. Alex couldn't begin to express how happy she was to see Myrddin. The worries she'd had before about Myrddin holding back information or keeping her on the outside had been dispelled. "Glad you found time in your busy schedule to stop by."

Myrddin conjured a cup of tea and offered it to Alex. "Not a problem. The dragonriders are my pet project. I believe you and the DGA are tied for the most time I spend. The Riders are far too valuable a project to allow someone else to oversee."

"How many different groups are there?"

Myrddin scrunched his face as he counted. "Far too many to name. The DGA and the Riders are my primary human projects. The MERC program is another one close to my heart since it holds the most humans throughout any corps, but that runs predominately on its own. It's a huge group. Has a pretty solid infrastructure. Then there are a handful throughout the nine realms that I run with different racial delegations and the like."

"Racial delegations?"

Myrddin finished his tea and placed the cup on the table next to Alex. "It is not my place to determine how any of the realms deal with the Dark One. That has been a problem in the past. It was one of the reasons the gnomish world fell. My predecessors showed up and informed the gnomes they were going to tell them how to defeat the Dark One. In many ways, it seemed like an invasion of another kind. I've learned from their mistakes."

Alex blew on her tea to cool it down. "How do you handle that now?"

"Slowly. With patience and understanding. But war politics isn't why I'm here. I came to see how you were doing."

"You came just to visit me?"

Myrddin was examining Alex's wheelchair as if he were looking for things to improve. "No, not to visit *only* you. Although you are the leader of Boundless, I have a lot riding on all of you. Jim is the youngest human mech rider. Jollies is perhaps our most proficient rider. The drow have only allowed one of their own to participate in the joint war efforts."

Alex leaned forward and asked, "What about Brath? What's your interest in him?"

Myrddin's brow furrowed and grew dark as his eyes sharpened. "Brath. Sometimes we hold our failures more closely than our successes. If you don't mind, I'd rather not talk about him. Lest you worry, he is just as exceptional as the rest of you."

Alex thought it better to keep from probing. "You talk to anyone else yet?"

Myrddin nodded slowly. "First, the dragons. They are all recovering well. Chine will have to spend more time under observation than the rest. We thought the same would be said of you. Of the Riders, Jollies is the one having the hardest time. Her bone density wasn't properly accounted for. She's on bed rest in the medbay for the next two days."

For all the irritation Myrddin had caused Alex recently, she was glad he had checked on her team. It let her know he cared. At times like this, Alex thought, that was the most important thing. "Itching to get your hands on that weapon?" Alex asked.

Myrddin looked solemn as if this was a question he'd been contemplating his entire life, and he was preparing to give the proper answer. "We're waiting until all the riders can be present. You risked your life for this. We should wait until you're all ready. Until then, at the request of your teammates, we're providing a…movie day. I believe that was what Jim called it."

If Alex could have, she would have leaped out of bed. "Are you serious?"

Myrddin jumped back a little bit, caught off-guard by Alex's excitement. "Uh, yes. He thought you might enjoy it a lot."

Alex didn't want to tell Myrddin, but since she'd gotten her eyes, she had been wanting to watch a movie. She'd spent much of her childhood listening to movies her father wanted to watch with her.

Myrddin stood and got ready to leave. "Also, one of the DGA agents has leave now as well. She should be arriving within the hour. Abby. I hope you all hit it off."

If Myrddin hadn't been in the room, Alex would have jumped for joy. Also, she had to be able to move comfortably. But she wanted to maintain some kind of professionalism, and she couldn't move much. "Great. Can't wait to see everyone."

Team Boundless was wheeled into Alex's barracks a few hours later. Everyone was complaining, Brath more than anyone else. A couple of strings had been pulled, and Jollies was brought into the barracks as well. After Boundless got settled, Abby arrived. She stood in the corner of the barracks for a bit after the soldiers left the room, not knowing whether she was going to talk to anyone. When Alex finally noticed her, she waved for Abby to come into the room.

Abby walked slowly as if uncertain if she should be included in the events, but Alex patted her bed multiple times to let her know she should feel comfortable enough to take a seat. Within minutes, Alex, Jollies, Abby, and Gill were in a heated debate over which movie they should watch.

Despite Alex's protests, they ended up watching a new elvish movie that Gill convinced Jim and Brath was worth viewing.

Needless to say, none of the humans were prepared for their first forays into elvish cinema. To begin with, there was hardly any dialogue. Most of the movie took place in a forest, with long shots meandering through trees. After the first hour, Abby finally convinced everyone to try another movie.

They eventually settled on an old film about a group of dwarves and halflings and elves making a journey against insurmountable odds. Alex was ecstatic about the choice. It was one of her parents' favorite films. She wished she was watching it with them, but she was glad her first movie experience was being shared with her teammates.

From there, they watched movies far into the night. The soldiers arranged for an additional bed to be put in for Abby and for Jollies' medbay setup to be brought into the room.

For the first time in a while, Alex forgot she was a soldier. She, Abby, and Jollies stayed up late, talking about whatever dropped into their minds. Alex would have been hard-pressed to remember the conversations, yet they felt more important than anything going on in the world at the moment.

Alex didn't know when she fell asleep, but it was the most peaceful repose she'd had in a long time.

CHAPTER EIGHT

The briefing took place at nine in the morning after the two-day leave. Team Boundless was rested, having enjoyed the brief period of normalcy. They were allowed to be teenagers for a bit, and even Brath seemed like he had benefited from not thinking about war 24/7.

Unfortunately, things had to return to normal, and Alex could see the disappointment on her team's face. For two days, they hadn't talked about the Dark One, read anything about battle tactics, or been drilled on flying exercises. They'd visited their dragons, but the beasts were still resting as well.

The briefing was a reminder that this was just a break.

Abby accompanied Boundless to the briefing. She wanted to get information on the weapon that was being used and take it back to the DGA base. They would run tests and do research. If she skipped out on the briefing, she would have to wait for secondhand information. "Don't make sense to wait around when I'm right here," she had said.

There were no disagreements. Abby was part of the Middang3ard efforts, even if she was in another department.

Jim mentioned that was something the military had problems with. You almost never saw government agencies working with each other. Maybe that was why Myrddin's system worked so well.

The briefing was to take place in the quarantine area of the base, which was where the shard was being kept. Alex wondered whether that was where Vardis was being kept as well. She doubted it. Even if she had her suspicions about Vardis, it wouldn't have sent the alien the right message.

As Boundless made their way toward the quarantine area, Jollies floated around Alex's head, complaining. "We should have more days like this. The last time we got a day off, it was a national holiday. And then this whole thing happened. It wasn't even a full day off."

Alex swatted Jollies away. "That's why we got two full days. It's not like you can just call a timeout in a war. If we're needed, we're needed. When was the last time you had a day off, Abby?"

Abby wasn't listening. She was looking down at her datapad as she was walking. "Hm… What was that? I was running diagnostics on your arm. There might be things I can upgrade so it runs a little smoother."

Jollies giggled as she flew over to Abby. "Doesn't look like she takes a break even on her days off. She was up all last night working."

Abby shrugged as her nano-parts absorbed the datapad back into her body. "I don't need as much sleep as I used to," she explained. "Part of being a cyborg, I guess. Didn't wanna keep everyone up by blabbing. Used to hate when my sisters did that."

Brath, who had returned to his usual disgruntled demeanor, caught up with the girls. "Glad to hear you didn't. Jim and Gill wouldn't shut up last night."

Gill and Jim exchanged glances that hinted they might be

hiding something. "It was a riveting game of chess," Gill said. "One that went on for far too long. Alex, you are lucky you made us take it outside."

Jim clapped Gill on the back and laughed. "Yeah, it took like six hours or something. And Gill doesn't believe in trash-talking during games of strategy. I had to teach him a lesson or two."

"Your trash-talking didn't help you win."

Jim strolled away nonchalantly. "Yeah, but it did make it harder for you to win. You gotta admit that."

"True. Perhaps that counts as a strategy. Wouldn't say it's a winning strategy, though."

Abby laughed at Jim's and Gill's banter. "Kinda nice to be 'round folks my age," she said between giggles. "Everyone's so serious at DGA. I think Anabelle's the only one who ever laughs."

Alex wracked her mind, trying to remember the names of everyone she had met on their mission with the DGA. "That's the elf, right?"

"Yeah. She's cool. Really cool. I like her a lot. I mean, as a teacher or whatever. But, yeah. It's a pretty serious place."

The kids arrived at the quarantine area, and the soldiers guarding the office let them in. Myrddin was already in the room, as were Vardis and Roy, the latter doing a double-take when he saw Abby. "Aren't you supposed to be at the DGA? Don't tell me you can teleport now with those nano-bots."

Abby shook her head as she walked farther into the room, which was separated from the shard by a thick sheet of glass. "Got a couple of days off. You might want to try it sometime. My pa used to say you can work a horse to death but then all ya got is a dead horse."

"Your country wisdom gets more morbid each week, you know?"

Abby peered through the glass to get a better look at the shard. "Just savin' the best ones for last."

Alex went up to the glass to look at the shard as well. "So, you said you wanted to wait until we were all here to talk about the shard, right?" she asked.

As Myrddin prepared to speak, Alex looked inward and found her voice, turning it outward and projecting it at Abby. *Hey, don't react. At all. Otherwise they'll know what I'm doing. But can you hear me? Answer or rest your right pinky on the glass.*

Alex didn't hear a response, but Abby did place her right pinky on the glass. She kept her eyes trained on the shard.

Alex nearly jumped out of her skin with excitement. *Perfect! Okay, it might be weird to talk back while trying to listen, but that shard looks just like the last one, doesn't it? Like it's made out of the same stuff the Dark One was using to separate us from our dragons.*

Abby's voice came through, small and squeaky as if it were uncertain of itself. *Yeah. I'm running a diagnostic. They look to have the same basic mineral structure, but I'll have to get my hands on it to pull a sample.*

Can you do that?

Abby tapped her pinky on the glass. No one could have seen it but Alex, whose dragon eyes magnified everything. A single nano-bot crept out from under Abby's nail and jumped onto the glass, cut a nano-bot sized hole, and went for the shard. *Don't worry, it'll seal everything up when it's done,* Abby assured Alex.

Alex and Abby turned around to face Myrddin, who was waiting for everyone's full attention. "This is less a briefing and more a meeting," Myrddin explained. "I'm glad Abby-Lynn could join us as well. Her knowledge always proves to be invaluable."

Abby modestly waved away Myrddin's compliment, conjuring old Southern manners into Alex's mind from books she'd read in braille. "Hardly. Don't know much about alien tech yet."

"I believe you said the same thing about gnomish aqueduct restoration last week, as well, a topic Brath would no doubt want to hear about at some point. But on to business. The shard, a weapon Vardis proposes we use to destroy the Dark One once and for all, has been retrieved. Vardis, would you care to explain how this weapon would do that?"

Vardis stood and walked toward the shard. He rested his hand on the glass, and Alex hoped that Abby's nano-bot had returned. She also made sure she was guarding her thoughts. "The dragonriders witnessed a fraction of what the shard was capable of on the moon. The defense matrix used—"

Brath cleared his throat loudly. "Oh, yeah, the matrix that malfunctioned and almost killed all of us. How did that happen again?"

Vardis slowly turned, his eyes neutral, and an apologetic smile crept across his face. "The system was hacked from off-site. If anyone had managed to get as close as we did, they would have been killed. I'm surprised we survived. But you can at least attest to the power of the weapon."

Gill raised his hand as if he were in a classroom. "This is a meeting, correct? We are all welcome to share our opinion?"

Roy good-naturedly nodded. "If you have something to say, get it out. This ain't that rank B.S. You guys were on the ground floor. We need to hear what you have to say."

Gill stood, his calmness wielded like a weapon. "We saw an attack by the Dark One's ship that looked capable of taking us out in one blow. The shard weapon defense wasn't able to stop five riders, and we were operating in a very limited manner. How would this weapon be able to destroy the Dark One if it could hardly handle us?"

Alex could have kissed Gill. She wouldn't have, but she could have. With everything that had been going on, Alex hadn't had a chance to stop and ask herself how a weapon that couldn't handle the dragonriders could handle the Dark One.

Vardis didn't seem perturbed by the question. "Ah, a good observation. Simply put, the weapon was also under a handicap. It was only using 0.05% of its energy. The defense that was summoned would be akin to your dragon batting its eyelash to shoo a fly. Outside the defense matrix, the weapon will operate at 100%."

Gill glanced at Myrddin, looking somewhat disappointed by the answer. "Will you explain to us exactly how this weapon works?" the wizard asked.

Vardis pressed his hand to the glass, and the shard began to glow. "Your team witnessed it firsthand. The shard is capable of summoning constructs from my dimension. The constructs take on the physical properties of whatever is used to summon them. They are nearly impossible to destroy at full power, but their true potential is in their volume. Millions of kin can be summoned at a time—a force to easily overrun the Dark One's."

Myrddin ran his long fingers through his silver beard. "What are these kin?"

Vardis turned away from the glass, and the shard ceased glowing. "They are biological constructs engineered in my dimension for the sole purpose of war. Elementals. One of the reasons they could be defeated was due to them being forged of rock, the weakest of elements. But if we were to use fire—a volcano on Middang3ard, for instance—they'd be unstoppable."

Roy scoffed as he folded his arms. "You're saying your weapon is an army. You think we should give you the resources to build an unstoppable army? For all we know, you could be just as bad as the Dark One. The only difference is his army isn't made up of hyperdimensional elementals, just flesh and blood like the rest of us."

Vardis' eyes darkened in that way only Alex seemed to notice. Even if she hadn't, she could feel the hatred coming off of Vardis. It hit her hard. This time he wasn't trying to hide it. Even if anyone else in the room didn't have telepathy, there was no way they couldn't sense this.

When Vardis spoke, you could hear the rage in his voice. "The Dark One took everything from me. I am nothing like him. Once he is destroyed, I want nothing else. You can keep the damn shard."

Roy backed off, and Vardis relaxed. "Besides," the alien went on. "'Unstoppable' is just semantics. The kin can't be defeated, but they have a limited life span. That's their failsafe. They have to be implemented wisely in a decisive battle, one where the Dark One is exposed. They only live for so long."

There was silence in the room while everyone weighed what had been said. The more Vardis had explained, the more of a gamble this sounded like. The decision was not straightforward.

Myrddin sat down and crossed his legs. "If it is amenable to the rest of you, I'd like to discuss and come to a final decision with Roy. That is unless any of you have a strong opinion about our next course of action?"

The members of Boundless looked at each other. Jim finally spoke. "We all trust Alex enough for this. Just let us know what's coming next."

"Thank you. You are all dismissed."

As Boundless and Vardis left, Abby walked past Alex and said, "Catch up with you later."

The two hugged quickly, and Alex whispered, "Yeah, see you in a bit."

Alex and Roy took seats across from Myrddin, who was

deep in thought. Roy, on the other hand, looked as if he hadn't been paying attention to the whole conversation. "Thoughts?" Alex asked.

Roy hardly seemed able to hold himself back when he spoke. "I think it's a real friggin' stupid idea. Give an unknown quantity control of an entire army. He didn't mention anything about how he was going to control them. How we were going to. All he mentioned was a time failsafe, and he neglected to say how long that time limit was. I think it's a crap idea. We should ditch it and destroy the shard."

Myrddin nodded as he listened to Roy. "What do you think, Alex?"

Alex had mentioned she had spoken with the Dark One in her initial debriefing. It wouldn't come as a surprise to Myrddin or Roy. "The Dark One seems pretty intent on stopping this weapon from being used. He said it was because it would destroy all life. I don't know if that's true, but he was willing to let Boundless live as long we kept the weapon from being used. We know he's afraid of it, at least."

Myrddin sighed as he hung his head, looking more tired every moment. "I do not like unknown quantities. We now know the Dark One fears this weapon, at least."

Alex felt a coldness in her heart over what she was about to say. "We should use the weapon. If Vardis tries anything, we kill him. It's that simple. Even if he raises his own army, what good is it without a leader?"

Roy seemed to be thinking the same thing. "A little ruthless. Definitely not something he'd be expecting from a bunch of kids. I'm in."

Myrddin slowly stood, taking his time since his body was creaking. "Then it's decided. We'll prep the collider for your return trip to Middang3ard. Then we will start looking for a viable place to use the weapon. Until then, you have a little more time off."

CHAPTER NINE

The members of Boundless all had different ideas of what "time off" meant. Almost immediately after the meeting, Gill and Jollies separated from the rest of the squad, practically locking themselves in the barracks to binge-watch any form of human entertainment they could get their hands on. After watching an elvish movie, Alex could see why.

Brath couldn't stay still, and he didn't want anyone's company. Alex had tried multiple times to talk to Brath or spend some time with him. As usual, he was bristly and untalkative. Unless it had to do with taking down the Dark One, he didn't seem interested in discussing it. The exception was his mistrust of Vardis.

Alex could see similarities between Vardis and Brath, but she was honestly surprised by how different they were. It was no secret that Brath was obsessed with the Dark One's destruction. He didn't mention it often, but when he did, it was obvious that it was on his mind all the time.

Vardis held the same desire, but the motivation was different. Alex had only heard Vardis speak about how much he wanted to kill the Dark One. Brath had many reasons, the one brought up the most being his love for his homeworld. Alex could easily tell Brath was concerned about his people being free and having a home again. His hatred for the Dark One was incidental.

Vardis had mentioned a few times that the Dark One had taken everything from him. Alex was curious about what he had taken from the alien.

Jim could hardly be found. He spent most of his time wandering through the hallways of the military base. Even though Alex tried to talk to him a few times, he seemed distant. Something was on his mind, and it wasn't anything he was willing to talk about.

So, Alex spent most of her time waiting with Abby. Neither of them had any problem with that. Abby had woken Alex up at the crack of dawn to rush her to the medbay to take a look at her cybernetics.

Alex was initially annoyed since she was not a morning person. When she saw how happy Abby was to have a chance to look at her arm, she couldn't stay angry. They spent most of the morning with Abby running tests on the arm, trying to find different augments she could add to beef it up.

By the time Abby was done, Alex's arm was not only running smoother but also had the addition of a small plasma cannon that operated using the draconic fluid running through Alex's veins.

When Abby was done working on Alex's arm, she leaned back and started checking through her notes. "So, what's the deal with this draconic fluid?" she asked. "You know exactly what it's doing?"

Alex tried to find the words to explain it to Abby. "It's their blood or their life force. The augments tear into their bodies, and the fluid comes out like pus. If it's left on their skin or they have too much inside, it sears through. So, the anchors absorb the fluid and convert it to energy."

Abby was listening intently, yet her eyes never left the computer screen. "Okay, I got that. Your anchor should be processing the fluid. Why is it in your blood and no one else's?"

"That is the real question. I haven't been given a straight answer. Makes me think it's not a common thing. I haven't been able to find any information about it in our books, either. Part of me thinks no one has told me anything about it because they haven't seen it before."

Abby turned to face Alex and held out her hand. Her nano-bots poured out of her pores and started to build a small tracking device. "Could I install this in your arm? Just as a way to keep track of the fluids in your blood so we can get a better idea about what's going on. I can tell you from experience, you shouldn't have things messing with your body that you don't know about."

"What do you mean?"

Abby's skin shifted from its usual dark brown to a metallic black. "I injected myself with nano-bots when I first started with the DGA. Now I have an AI living in my brain, and I'm not sure if the nano-bots are trying to replace all of my organic material or not. They don't talk."

Alex had never thought there might be a negative effect of the draconic fluid. She believed Chine would have told her if that was the case. Maybe he didn't know. "You think something bad might happen?"

Abby's skin returned to normal as she shook her head. "Nah, not really. But I thought the same thing when I pumped myself full of robots. Might be better to be safe than sorry."

"Won't those try to infect me?"

"Nah. These bots are tuned to my body. Once they're out,

they're just standard constructions. No will or anything. But I thought I should ask before adding stuff to your body."

Alex gave Abby her hand. "Thanks for that."

Abby installed the tracker in Alex's arm. After she was finished, the rider stood and stretched. "Ugh, we've been in here all day. Let's go for a walk or something. Maybe grab some food."

Alex's stomach gurgled loudly, and Abby laughed at the sound. "I always forget to eat." She chuckled. "Don't get hungry much anymore. Nanobots are always trying to make my body more efficient."

"You still like food, though, right?"

Abby smiled devilishly. "Oh, wait until you see me eat."

The scientist hadn't been lying. Alex watched Abby put away two lunches and three rounds of dessert. Abby didn't talk when she ate, she merely inhaled her food. Alex didn't know whether to be grossed out or amused.

When Abby finally finished eating, she let out a small belch and leaned back in her chair. "Sorry. I haven't had human food made by humans in a *long* time. Makes a huge difference. Ain't as good as the fam's, but it's close."

Alex snatched a leftover biscuit from Abby's plate. "You could still eat more, couldn't you?"

Abby patted her stomach as she smiled. "Best part of having nanobots regulate your body. They compensate for everything."

Suddenly Abby's face went serious. "Got something on my mind, though. That guy, Vardis. What're your thoughts on him?"

Alex wasn't sure if she should disclose her mistrust of Vardis to Abby. Boundless and Myrddin knew, but that was because they had been on the mission. Anything else might have just been putting people on edge unnecessarily. "He says he has a weapon that'll take care of the Dark One. What more do we need to know?"

Abby was silent for a moment, looking as if she were trying to find the right words to express her worries. "Took a quick look last night. There are only a couple of volcanoes in Middang3ard. The biggest ones, which would yield the largest number of kin, have channels that lead to the core of the planet. And I know Myrddin—he'll want to go big or go home. That's what he'll give Vardis."

Alex poked the leftover food on her plate. "You think he'll do it even if he has cause not to trust Vardis?"

Abby nodded solemnly. "He's a gambler. Might put on an air of being in control and whatnot, but he doesn't know what's going on any more than the rest of us most of the time. He just does a better job of hiding it. He's as likely to risk it all as any of us are."

Alex weighed her options. There didn't seem to be many. "Okay. I'll have Gill and Jim take a look at prospective places. Tomorrow. I don't want to deal with it until tomorrow. I want a normal night, or as normal as it can get."

"What's the most normal thing you can think of?"

Alex ran a couple of scenarios in her head. "You want to come to dinner with Jim and me?"

CHAPTER TEN

Dinner was served at 6:30, which was earlier than Alex was used to. For the last few weeks, she'd been able to eat anytime she wanted to. Being restricted to her parents' idea of when food should be served was interesting, to say the least.

Jim and Abby showed up at her door a little before the food was to be served. Her parents were caught off-guard by two additional people arriving for dinner but didn't say anything.

Alex brought Abby and Jim into the kitchen, fielding questions from her parents that she didn't want to deal with. Most of them had to do with Alex's mission. Her father was very curious to know how it had all panned out. Alex wasn't ready to give them any details.

Jim and Abby did most of the talking during the meal prep. Alex's parents were more than happy to be regaled with Abby's stories of the bizarreness of working with so many non-humans. They were equally interested in Jim's tales of being the only mech rider in Boundless.

Alex stayed quiet and helped with the preparations as

much as she could. It was a pleasant change to be told what to do rather than having to make the calls herself, even if the decisions were as benign as choosing the proper way to cut an onion.

Chicken curry was what Alex's father had planned for the evening. After all the ingredients had been sliced and diced appropriately, Claire had said she'd watch the pot while everyone else waited in the living room.

An awkward silence fell over Alex and the rest as they tried to think of a conversation point. Finally, Alex remembered the videos she'd recorded of her flight out to space. She pulled up her HUD and transferred the files to the smart TV in the living room.

To say Alex's father was impressed by the videos would have been an understatement. He was speechless for most of the time he was watching. When the footage of the moon came up, he lost his mind and giggled like a child, almost jumping out of his seat.

Alex was glad she'd remembered to bring this part of her life home to her dad. When dinner was finally served, it took everything in Claire's power to bring her husband to the table. Once they were all seated, space was the topic of utmost importance.

Anything to keep from talking about what was actually going on. Alex was glad her parents were getting along with Abby and Jim. Both of them avoided intrusive questions, more than happy to try to have a normal night at home.

And for the most part, it was normal. So normal that Alex wondered why she had ever gotten involved with Myrddin and this fight against the Dark One. This would have been more than enough to keep her happy for the rest of her life.

That was what she'd like to tell herself, but deep down, she knew that wasn't true. Her mind hadn't left the issue of the shard since she'd set foot in her home.

It was nice to pretend there were things outside of the Dark One and his war, but Alex knew the truth. Even these simple interactions with her family and friends were shaped by her knowledge that there was a force trying to enslave everyone in existence, and there was another that was possibly trying to end them.

All in all, Alex appreciated the break. She didn't talk much during dinner, choosing instead to listen to the surrounding conversation. Everyone seemed to be having a good time.

Once dinner was over, her parents cleared the table, leaving Alex, Abby, and Jim alone. Even though the meal and family time had gone surprisingly well, none of the three seemed particularly settled or comfortable. Jim was the one to broach the awkwardness. "Are we going to talk about Vardis?" he asked.

Alex was preparing to say something when Abby interrupted her. "I'm not part of your team, I know, but I don't trust him. Don't know if it's my place to say, but I'm not about this."

Jim and Alex exchanged glances. Nothing more needed to be said. They were all on the same page. "Hey," Alex said, "how about we go help out with dishes?"

With that, the three slipped into a visage of normalcy that continued until the dining room and kitchen were clean and Jim and Abby were picked up by members of Earth's HQ to take them back to the base. The goodbyes were swift, lacking in affection, and sterile.

Alex wished they had headed out on a better note, but she realized they all had something on their minds. After Jim and Abby left, Alex returned to the living room. Her parents were sitting and talking quietly, only stopping for a second when Alex came in. She could read the room. She figured it was best for her to go to bed.

Nostalgia hit Alex like a train when she walked into her

bedroom. She couldn't remember the last time she'd been in her own room. It seemed like an entirely different dimension, far removed from the Wasps Nest. She felt more alien in here than in her dorm room at the Nest.

Regardless, the room still made her sleep. She slipped into her bed without a second thought and found herself dozing off almost instantly. Her eyes were heavy, and she couldn't keep them open. Slowly closing...drifting away.

When Alex opened her eyes, she was in a white plane, one that she knew. In the distance, she saw someone working, their back turned to her.

It was Vardis. She recognized the feeling of the place. It was the same plane he had drawn her into before. The only difference this time was that Vardis wasn't aware she was there. Alex decided to take advantage of the moment. She snuck up behind Vardis, hiding her thoughts and making sure he didn't notice her.

When Alex reached Vardis' shoulder and was able to peek over and see what he was working on, she was gripped with a fear she'd never known her entire life. A fear that far surpassed anything the Dark One had ever incurred within her.

She beheld what lay in Vardis' palms and trembled.

Then Alex was flung into the darkness of her dreams, to try to make sense of what she'd seen upon waking.

Death is coming ... but can Alex stop it? And at what cost?

AUTHOR NOTES RAMY VANCE

MAY 2, 2020

So my latest launch was held up in Amazon's processing center. For days! Eight to be exact. It seems the Dark Gate Angels (a new Middang3ard series) was just too much for Amazon to handle.

That or they were short staffed due to Covid-19 … I like to think it was the book being too epic.

Regardless of the reason (too hot to handle), those eight days were filled with me refreshing my Amazon page a million times, yelling at my computer while I anxiously waited for my latest release to go live.

In my frustration, I made these:

Hey, if you can't have passive aggressive fun with your frustrations, what else is there to do?

I made a couple others, but Michael – for legal reasons – forbade me from sharing them!

AUTHOR NOTES MICHAEL ANDERLE

MAY 17, 2020

THANK YOU for reading our story!

We have a few of these planned, but we don't know if we should continue writing and publishing without your input.

Options include leaving a review, reaching out on Facebook to let us know, and smoke signals.

Frankly, smoke signals might get misconstrued as low hanging clouds, so you might want to nix that idea...

A Radio Interview... How novel!

So, this Sunday, I am going to be interviewed by a local radio station in Savannah, GA for a couple of hours. Frankly, I'm trying to figure out what we are going to talk about.

The host of the show, Adam Messler, promises me we can fill two hours, and I'm going to go with that since I'm not sure. He's the expert, not me.

One of the interesting aspects of this interview is that we will have it using a phone. After the last couple of months (and frankly, for a few years now), I almost NEVER use the phone for any type of business communication.

Except to call our insurance agent or his team.

I'm scratching my head, thinking about what it will feel like to go old-school and just *talk*. I won't have to worry about shaving (YEAH!) or what I'm wearing or anything (Is my office clean? It won't matter, we aren't on video.).

I expect to enjoy myself, as long as there isn't a bunch of dead air space where I don't know what to say.

Don't Let Ramy Get Bored...and exasperated.

I don't want to say too much about Ramy's frustration with our last book that came out.

It was during a really hard to for Amazon (for some reason—Amazon doesn't share what happens even if thousands have felt it or seen the problems. It is kinda like the US Government "No, those lights up in the sky we chased with jets? It was swamp gas... Wait, ball lightning!")

When Ramy goes too far into bored and exasperated, waiting for the book to be released after days and days, he gets feisty.

Ad Aeternitatem,

Michael Anderle

OTHER BOOKS BY THE AUTHORS

Other Middang3ard Books

Never Split The Party (01)
Late To the Party (02)
It's My Party (03)
Blue Hell And Alien Fire (04)

Death Of An Author: A Middang3ard Novella

Dark Gate Angels

Other Books by Ramy Vance

Mortality Bites Series
Keep Evolving Series
Fatebound Series
Welcome to the Dragon Show Series

Other Books by Michael Anderle

CONNECT WITH THE AUTHORS

Connect with Ramy

Join Ramy's Newsletter to get a **FREE AUDIOBOOK!**
Join Ramy's FB Group: House of the GoneGod Damned!

Connect with Michael Anderle and sign up for his email list here:

Website: http://lmbpn.com

Email List: http://lmbpn.com/email/

Facebook:
www.facebook.com/TheKurtherianGambitBooks